This book

This is the story of Goldilocks,

a little girl who never knocks.

And on every page there's

a clock to spot!

Goldilocks
and the
Three Bears

Nick and Claire Page

Illustrations by Sara Baker

make
believe
ideas

In a house in the woods, lived Daddy Bear,
married to Mom with curly hair.
Smallest of all, in the rocking chair,
is their baby, Little Bear Bottom.

8

It's breakfast time, believe it or not!
The porridge is done, but it's way too hot!
So they go for a walk,
while it cools in the pot –
Mom, Dad, and Little Bear Bottom.

Along comes a girl called Goldilocks,
wearing her favorite red and blue socks.
She walks straight in — the girl never knocks!
Her manners are gone. She forgot 'em!

10

She looks for some porridge, and, guess what!
One's too cold, and one's too hot.
The last is just right, she gobbles the lot.
What a bad little girl — she's rotten!

Feeling full up, she wants to sit down.
"Too hard! Too soft!" she says with a frown.
Tries baby bear's chair, and ends upside down!
Crash! She's gone through the bottom!

Sleepy, she goes upstairs to bed.
Too high, too low, two beds hurt her head.
So she picks the little bear's bed instead.
(She likes the sheets, they are cotton.)

The bears come home. The bears are mad!

"Someone's been eating my porridge," says Dad.

"Mine too," says Mom,

"And mine," says their lad.

"She's eaten it right to the bottom!"

"Someone's been sitting in my chair, too,"
says Dad, then Mom, "Oh, what shall we do?"
"And mine is broken. Boo hoo! It was new!"
cries sad little Baby Bear Bottom.

20

They race up the stairs, and hearing a knock,
Goldilocks suddenly wakes with a shock!
Little Bear screams, and she's up like a shot,
"There's the intruder — we've got 'em!"

Out of the window she jumps – and away!
She learns a lot about bears that day –
their beds, their chairs, and to stay far away
from the porridge of Baby Bear Bottom!

Ready to tell

Oh no! Some of the pictures from this story have been mixed up! Can you retell the story and point to each picture in the correct order?

Picture dictionary

Encourage your child to read these words from the story and gradually develop his or her basic vocabulary.

bear

bed

breakfast

broken

chair

hot

porridge

scream

walk

Key words

Here are some key words used in context. Help your child to use other words from the border in simple sentences.

Breakfast **is** ready.

Goldilocks eats **the** porridge.

She breaks the chair.

She sleeps **in** the bed.

Goldilocks runs **away.**

Make yummy porridge!

Goldilocks loved the three bears' porridge. Try making some yourself from this delicious traditional porridge recipe from Scotland.

You will need

1 cup oatmeal • 4 cups cold water • $\frac{1}{2}$ tsp salt
• 2 tsp sugar • $\frac{1}{2}$ cup buttermilk or cream

What to do

1 Put the oatmeal into a saucepan with the cold water.

2 Stir gently over a medium heat until the mixture starts to boil.

3 Lower the heat and continue to stir – to avoid any lumps – for five minutes. The mixture will become thick and creamy.

4 Add the salt, sugar, and buttermilk or cream.

5 Give the porridge a final stir and serve hot.

Porridge tastes great with:

- raspberries
- maple syrup and whipped cream
- chocolate raisins
- raisins and cinnamon
- apple sauce and cinnamon
- sliced bananas